Incy Wincy Spider

Written by Catherine Baker

Illustrated by Andrea Castro Naranjo

Collins

2

4

6

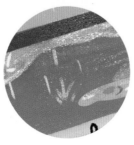

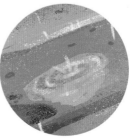

8

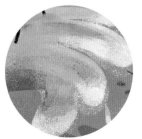

9

10

12

Where did Incy Wincy go?
What did he do?

 After reading

Letters and Sounds: Phase 1

Word count: 0

Curriculum links: EYFS: Understanding the World: The World

Early learning goals: Listening and attention: children listen attentively in a range of situations; Understanding: children answer 'how' and 'why' questions about their experiences and in response to stories or events

Developing fluency

- Encourage your child to hold the book and turn the pages.
- Ensure that your child understands that the book is about the Incy Wincy Spider rhyme and that they can recognise the elements from the rhyme on each page. (e.g. *the rain, the sun*)
- Look at the pictures together and encourage your child to talk about what is happening in each one, giving as much detail as they can. What creatures can they see? What are they doing? What is the weather like and how is it changing?

Phonic practice

- Together, look for objects in the pictures that make sounds. (e.g. *the minibeasts, the animals, the rain*)
- Look for opportunities to explore alliteration, by focusing on things in the pictures that begin with 'b' on pages 2–3, 'c' on pages 4–5, 'r' on pages 6–7, 'w' on pages 8–9, 's' on pages 10–11 and pages 12–13.

Extending vocabulary

- Talk about the pictures in circles at the bottom of the pages. Ask your child to tell you what they see. Can they spot the objects in the main picture?
- Discuss words for all of the minibeasts and other things in the pictures.
- Talk about words for the weather. (e.g. *rainy, sunny*) For each weather type, ask your child to think of words that describe what that weather type is like/feels like. (e.g. *rainy = wet, damp, cold, soaking; sunny = warm, hot*)